FAIRY TALE MIX-UPS

The Frog Prince
Saves
Sleeping Beauty

written by Charlotte Guillain
illustrated by Dan Widdowson

capstone

Once upon a time, a princess was born in a faraway land. The king and queen were so happy.

"Let's have a party," said the king.

"Yes!" said the queen. "We will invite three fairy **godmothers**."

3

The day of the party arrived. The *fairy* **godmothers** brought their magic wands.

SHAZAM! A sparkly tricycle appeared.

SHAZAM! There was a shiny ball.

But just as the third *fairy* godmother waved her wand, the doors flew open.

"What's happening?" cried the king.

A wicked fairy flew into the room.

"You didn't invite me," she **cackled**. Everyone shivered with fear.

"My present for the princess is a **curse**," said the wicked fairy. "If the princess pricks her finger before she is ten years old, she will die."

SHAZAM!

Everyone **gasped**. The wicked fairy vanished.

"Help us, please!" the king and queen begged the fairy **godmothers**.

"I can't stop the **curse**," said the third fairy godmother. "But I can change it. If the princess pricks her finger, she will not die. She will just sleep until she is kissed by a prince."

After that, the king and queen kept the princess away from pins and needles.

"Play outside," they told her. "There are no pins in the garden."

The princess loved studying the flowers and birds. She loved watching the bees and butterflies.

One day, just before she turned ten years old, the princess found a frog. He looked so sweet.

The princess took the frog back to the palace and put him in a tank. The frog thought she was very kind.

The princess drew a picture of the frog. But just as she was pinning it on the wall ...

... the princess pricked her finger and fell asleep.

The *fairy* **godmothers** saw everyone in the palace was upset. They put them all to sleep too.

"If only a prince would come and kiss her," they sighed.

With everyone in the palace asleep, the frog was the only one left awake.

The *frog* saw that this was his chance. It was time *for* him to be a hero!

The *frog* hopped out of the tank and over to the princess's bed. Then he gave her a big, wet kiss.

When the princess woke up ...

... the *frog* turned into a prince!

"The wicked *fairy* turned me into a *frog*," he said. "The spell could only be broken if I kissed a princess."

"Thanks for saving me!" said the princess. The *fairy* **godmothers** shouted for joy and woke up everyone in the palace.

The princess and the prince became best friends. Together they looked after the animals in the palace garden.

Sleeping Beauty

The story of *Sleeping Beauty* was first written down by a French writer called Charles Perrault. In the story, a king and queen have a daughter and invite seven fairy **godmothers** to her christening. A wicked fairy bursts in and puts a **curse** on the baby. She will prick her finger on a **spindle** and die. The last fairy godmother casts her own spell that the princess will not die but will fall asleep for 100 years. Only a prince's kiss will wake her. The princess grows up, pricks her finger, and falls asleep. Luckily, a prince finds the palace and wakes Sleeping Beauty.

The Frog Prince

The Frog Prince was first written down by the Brothers Grimm. They lived in Germany 200 years ago. In the story, a princess drops her golden ball into a stream and meets a frog. The princess promises that if he gets her ball, he can live in the palace. But when he gets her ball, she runs away. The frog goes to the palace, and the king tells his daughter she must keep her word. The princess cares for the frog, and on the third day, the frog turns into a prince. He had been cursed by a wicked fairy.

Glossary

cackle—to laugh in an evil way

curse—a type of spell that will make bad things happen to someone

gasp—breathe in quickly in surprise

godmother—a person who promises to help bring up a child in a good way

spindle—something that thread is wound around when someone is spinning

Writing Prompts

Tell the story of what happens to the Frog Prince in his own words.

Write an invitation to the fairy godmothers asking them to come to the party.

Write a diary entry for the wicked fairy for the day of the party. How did she feel about not being invited?

Read More

Grimm, Jacob and Wilhelm, and Lewis, Naomi. *The Frog Prince*. New York: NorthSouth, 2013

Man-Kong, Mary. *Sleeping Beauty* (Step into Reading). New York: RH/Disney, 2014

Namm, Diane. *The Frog Prince* (Silver Penny Stories). New York: Sterling Children's Books, 2013

Speed Shaskan, Trisha. *Truly, We Both Loved Beauty Dearly!: The Story of Sleeping Beauty as Told by the Good and Bad Fairies* (The Other Side of the Story). North Mankato, MN: Picture Window Books, 2013

Internet sites

Facthound offers a safe, fun way to find web sites related to this book. All the sites on Facthound have been researched by our staff.

Here's all you do:
Visit **www.facthound.com**
Type in this code: 9781410983022

Read all the books in the series:

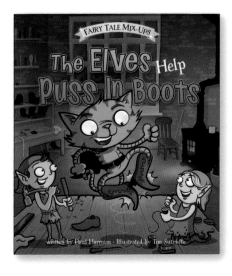

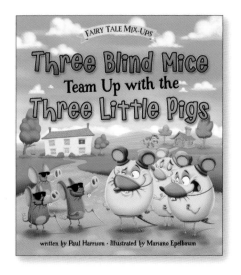

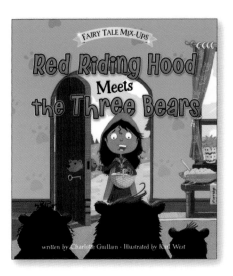

Visit www.mycapstone.com

Edited by Penny West
Designed by Steve Mead
Original illustrations © Capstone Global Library Ltd 2016
Illustrated by Dan Widdowson, The Bright Agency
Production by Steve Walker
Originated by Capstone Global Library Limited

Library of Congress Cataloging-in-Publication Data
Names: Guillain, Charlotte, author. | Widdowson, Dan, illustrator.
Title: Frog Prince saves Sleeping Beauty / by Charlotte Guillain ; [Dan Widdowson, illustrator].
Description: North Mankato, Minnesota : Heinemann-Raintree, an imprint of Capstone Press, [2017] | Series: Read and learn. Fairy tales mix-ups | Summary: "Sleeping Beauty is cursed to fall asleep, but is rescued by the frog prince who lives in the palace garden"-- Provided by publisher. Identifiers: LCCN 2015047491 | ISBN 9781410983022 (library binding) | ISBN 9781410983107 (pbk.) | ISBN 9781410983145 (ebook (pdf)) Subjects: | CYAC: Fairy tales. | Characters in literature--Fiction. | Princesses--Fiction. | Frogs--Fiction. | Blessing and cursing--Fiction. Classification: LCC PZ8.G947 Fro 2017 | DDC [E]--dc23 LC record available at https://lccn.loc.gov/2015047491

ISBN: 978-1-4109-8302-2 (library binding)
ISBN: 978-1-4109-8310-7 (paperback)
ISBN: 978-1-4109-8314-5 (eBook PDF)

Summary: Sleeping Beauty has been cursed to sleep until a prince kisses her. There are no princes in sight, but there is a frog in the palace garden. Can he help?

Printed and bound in the United States of America.
042017   010434RP